BEST
FRIENDS

BEST FRIENDS

CHRISTINE WRIGHT

Illustrated by Jane Kemp

Scripture Union
130 City Road, London EC1V 2NJ

By the same author
for older readers:
The Forbidden Mountain (Leopard Book)
Turnabout (Swift Books)
Coming Back
More than a Match

© Christine Wright 1989
First published 1989

ISBN 0 86201 553 7

Phototypeset by Input Typesetting Ltd, London SW19
Printed and bound in Great Britain by Cox and Wyman
Ltd, Reading

Contents

Just wait and see!

It was moving day for the Court family. Rosie felt as though she had a huge solid lump in her tummy. The house in which she had always lived was not home any more. It was just a bare, empty house.

Mum and Dad were busy with the removal men, trying to fit a few last things into the big blue van in the street.

'I think I'll go and say goodbye to the house,' Rosie said. But nobody heard her. Everyone else was staring hopelessly at a tray of plants that Mum held.

'Well, we can't take them on the train with us,' she was saying. Rosie noticed how excited she looked with her cheeks so pink and her curls poking out from under the scarf she had tied over her head to keep the dust off.

One of the removal men shook his head slowly. 'Should have packed them sooner, really,' he said. 'Don't blame me if they get broken.'

'I think I'll go and have one last look,' said Rosie a little louder.

Still nobody heard. So Rosie turned and went up the path between the colourful flower beds under the lilac trees to the front door and into the house. She climbed the bare, wooden staircase and went into the bedroom which she had shared with her younger brother, Mark.

Without beds and the carpet, without the wardrobe and the books on the window sill, without the clutter of toys and shoes on the floor, it didn't seem as though this had ever been her bedroom. Rosie stood twisting one of her brown plaits in her fingers, her freckled face long and sad.

'It isn't our house any more,' she said out loud. Her voice echoed round the empty room and made her feel even sadder. 'Goodbye,' she said, clattering downstairs again. 'Goodbye, house.'

A few minutes later, Mrs Green, their neighbour, was driving the Court family to the station in her car.

Rosie was squashed between Mum and Mark on the back seat of the car. Dad had to sit in the front seat, of course, because his legs were so long. As they drove away, people waved at them, all their friends who had come to see them off.

'Be sure to come back and see us, now!' someone said.

'Hope you like your new home!' shouted another voice.

'Bye! Goodbye!' they all called.

'Well,' said Dad as they turned the corner, 'wasn't that nice of them all? So many people to see us off.'

Rosie found that she couldn't see properly. Her eyes were full of tears. Beside her, curly-headed Mark was very quiet, which was most unusual.

Mum smiled at them. 'Cheer up,' she said kindly. 'I know it seems sad now, but our new house is very nice. We'll soon feel at home there. And, just think, you'll be

able to have a bedroom each now!'

'I like our old house,' sniffed Mark.

'And our old friends,' sighed Rosie.

'And our old school,' sobbed Mark.

'And our old church,' wept Rosie.

'We'll like our new things soon,' said Dad. 'Just wait and see. Before long, we'll be just as happy with our new house, our new friends and everything.'

Everyone was quiet during the long train journey, hardly talking, just staring out of the windows.

'Look,' said Dad as they were finishing the sandwiches they'd brought with them, 'we're nearly there! Can you see that big town up ahead? That's where we're going to live!'

Mark stood up to have a look, but Rosie turned away. 'Oh Mum,' she wailed miserably, 'I want to go home!'

'I know,' said Mum, giving her a hug, 'but we can't go back. Dad's got a job at last and we must be glad about that, even though it means we've got to move.'

'It will all be different, though,' said Rosie.

'Not everything,' Mum reminded her. 'We'll all be together still just the same, you and me, Mark and Dad. Best of all we'll still have our Father God to look after us. He'll never leave us. We'll be all right, Rosie.'

When the train stopped at the next station, the family climbed out on to a long platform. They'd arrived!

It was a pity to think that they had no friends to come and meet them. They stood in the street, looking down the hill at the town that was going to be their home. Rosie didn't much like what she saw.

All those grey houses in long, dark lines and we don't know anyone, not anyone that lives here, she thought.

'We'll get a taxi,' said Dad. 'I wonder whether the van's arrived at the new house yet.'

'It's sure to have,' Mum said. 'They'll be putting down the carpets, I expect.'

'Same carpets?' asked Mark.

'Yes, same carpets,' Dad said. 'Most of them, anyway.'

'Same chairs and table?' asked Mark.

'Yes, of course.'

'Same beds too?' he asked.

'Yes, yes!' laughed Dad. 'Everything the same. Just wait and see.'

Settling in

While Dad paid the taxi driver, Mark and Rosie stood in the street and looked around them. The blue removal van was half blocking the road outside a house which looked just the same as all the others in the street.

'We haven't got a garden,' said Mark. 'Just a door that opens and you're out on the pavement.'

'I can't see any trees or grass or flowers,' whispered Rosie. She didn't speak out loud because there were some children on the other side of the street and she didn't want them to hear. It was bad enough to have them staring at her like that. She glanced at them. There were several boys and girls who looked as though they all belonged to one family. They had brown skins and straight, shiny black hair. Rosie noticed their neat, brightly coloured clothes and wished that she and Mark weren't wearing their oldest trousers and T-shirts that had got grubby and crumpled.

'Come on,' called Mum from the doorway. 'Come and look inside.'

Mark followed Rosie in. At first glance, he didn't like the new house much. There were boxes lying everywhere and nowhere to sit except the floor. For a while, he wandered around, looking in each empty room and out of each curtainless window. Then he began to feel tired and settled down on the stairs to watch what was going on.

Before he'd been sitting there two minutes, though, one of the removal men came up carrying the bathroom cabinet.

'Shouldn't sit there, mate,' he said. 'You'll be right in the way.'

So Mark went into the bedroom that was going to be his. He could see everything that was going on in the street through the window. He leant against the wall, rested his elbows on the sill and settled down.

He'd hardly been there five minutes before his bed arrived, carried by two removal men.

'Sorry mate, better move for a while,' said one of them. And so it went on. Wherever he sat or stood, before long someone would want to move him.

'Mind out, now,' they'd say, or, 'Out of the way, please.' And Mark would have to find another place to go. He began to feel very cross.

Mum and Dad were getting tired and cross too.

'Keep out of the way, Mark,' they said. 'We're trying to get the bedrooms sorted out. Please don't stand just there.'

Mark yelled, 'I want my tea!'

Dad snapped, 'We all want our tea, but we've got to finish this first. Then we'll unpack the boxes in the kitchen. We can't have any tea until that's done.'

Mark stomped crossly downstairs and went to the kitchen. He looked around. On the floor there were five big boxes. These must be the ones that had to be unpacked before he could have his tea.

'Well,' he thought, 'Mum and Dad are busy upstairs, so I'd better empty them myself. That will save time later!'

He ripped the tape off the boxes, then began to unpack the first one. It was full of saucepans and dishes. Carefully, he took out each one and placed them all on the floor. The dishes were wrapped in newspaper. He unwrapped them and screwed the paper into balls.

In the second box, he found plates, cups and saucers which he piled up on the floor by the cupboards. There was so much newspaper in this box that he had to pile some of it on top of the saucepans.

In the third and fourth boxes, there were glasses, jugs, cleaning things and all sorts of jars, pots and pans. He took them out and put them on to the kitchen table, as there was no room on the floor.

At last, in the very last box, he found the food. It was hard work emptying this box. There were so many bits and pieces. He had to pile all the cans, tins and packets on the cooker, the draining boards and even in the sink as all the other spaces were filled already.

He'd almost finished when Mum came and stood in the doorway.

When she saw what he'd done, her eyes opened wide, but she didn't smile. She just sank down on to the floor and hid her head in her hands.

'Oh, Mark!' she cried. 'What have you been doing?'

He couldn't understand why she wasn't pleased that he had been so busy. Then he looked around and realized that Mum couldn't get into the kitchen. She couldn't even begin to start getting tea now. And he couldn't get out of the kitchen because he'd put piles of things all around him.

'I was trying to help,' he said in a small voice.

Mum looked up. 'I know,' she said wearily. 'But now I'm going to need a lot more help to get all this sorted out.'

Mark felt bad. His lip began to quiver the way it did just before he began to cry, but just then there was a knock at the front door. Dad and Rosie ran down the stairs to answer it.

'We'd better start on the kitchen,' said Mum, 'no matter who that is, or there won't be any tea today.'

Mark nodded and began to put all the newspaper into the empty boxes as Mum told him to. Quite quickly, the kitchen began to look better and Mum could get in to start finding cupboards for all the food.

They heard the front door shut and then Dad came out to the kitchen. He grinned, smoothing back his dark hair with grubby hands which left grey marks on his round, happy face.

'You can leave that,' he said. 'Guess what? That was one of our neighbours, Mrs Ram, from just over the road. Did you see her children out on the street when we arrived? She's cooking us a meal and she's invited us to go and eat with her family!'

'Oh!' sighed Mum. 'How wonderful!' And she smiled at Mark, her cheeks going pink with pleasure. He grinned back.

A couple of hours later, Mum, Mark and Rosie walked back across the street from the Rams'. Dad had already gone back to the new house with Mr Ram to get the bedrooms ready for the children.

Mark was happy. 'Guess what?' he asked. 'Sadhu's only two weeks older than me. He says he might be in my class at school and, Mum, guess what, he says when we go to church, he'll be there because the Rams go to church too!'

'I know,' said Mum, who'd heard it all before several

times. 'We can really thank God for the Rams. They're so kind to us. Mrs Ram has even promised to come and help me sort out the kitchen later.'

They stood outside the front door while Mum felt in her pocket for the key.

'Our new house,' sighed Mark. 'Just think, I've got a new house and a new friend all in one day. I think I'm going to like it here.'

A friend for Rosie

On Saturday afternoon, Rosie was staring out of her bedroom window. The rain was falling heavily on to the grey street, making little shiny puddles here and there.

'If it wasn't raining,' she thought, 'I could play in the garden.' There was a tiny garden behind the house, but because of the rain, Rosie hadn't been able to explore it yet.

She was bored. Mum came in and sat next to her for a moment. She glanced in Rosie's mirror and pushed back her curls with a little tired sigh.

'I've got nothing to do,' grumbled Rosie.

'I've got plenty to do,' said Mum. 'Why don't you come and help me?'

'I don't want to,' said Rosie miserably. 'I'm too tired.'

'Oh well,' sighed Mum. 'Perhaps you will later, then.'

She got off the bed and, in a few minutes, Rosie could hear that she was busy in the bathroom. Downstairs, Dad was fixing up some new shelves in the kitchen. Mark was out again, playing with his new friend, Sadhu.

'I'm the only one with nothing to do,' thought Rosie. 'If only I had a friend like Mark has.'

Rosie was bored all afternoon. She had spent a long time the day before getting her bedroom sorted out. She had arranged everything very neatly and, for the first time in her life, she had a bedroom that was really tidy. Her own bedroom! Every book was on the right shelf. Every toy was in the right place. Every ornament was on the right ledge. She was very proud of it. The trouble was that she was afraid of making it messy, so she didn't want to take anything out of its place. And so she had nothing to do.

All afternoon she sat on the bed, getting crosser and crosser. Mum and Dad were so busy. There was no one to play with. It wasn't fair! What a miserable day she was having!

'What is the matter?' asked Mum as she stomped down for her tea. They had to eat in the kitchen, perching on high stools because the only clear table was there. Rosie felt uncomfortable.

'Cheer up, Rosie,' said Dad as she sat down at the table. 'What's the cross face for?'

Rosie pouted. 'It's not fair,' she cried, 'Mark's got a friend already and I haven't. I've got nothing to do.'

'You could have gone to the Rams' with Mark,' Mum reminded her. 'And there's plenty to do here if you would only help.'

'But neither of Sadhu's sisters are old enough to play with me,' Rosie grumbled. 'And it's boring helping.'

'Not as boring as doing nothing, I should think,' said Mum.

Rosie frowned. She knew she'd been mean not to help Mum that afternoon. 'I'm sorry,' she said. 'Can I help you after tea?'

Mum smiled. 'Yes, of course. We can have some fun

together. You know that big cupboard under the stairs? Let's explore it properly and decide what to keep there, shall we?'

'And you'll soon find friends,' Dad told her. 'Give it a few more days. We've only been living here three days, after all!'

'And tomorrow is Sunday,' said Mum. 'Maybe you'll find a friend or two when we go to church.'

Next morning, Rosie looked around the church. It was a beautiful old building, smelling of polished wood and old books. The coloured windows hid the grey street outside. But, although Rosie loved the place at first sight, she was not happy. Something was wrong. There were people of all kinds there, just as there had been at their old church. The difference was that none of her friends was there. All the faces were strange to her. She didn't know anyone except the Rams and her own family.

She peeped around, trying to see everyone, but there didn't seem to be a girl of her own age. There were little girls and bigger girls and plenty of boys, but Rosie didn't think any of them would want to be friends!

Not fair! she thought. She couldn't think at all about God, although she knew that was why she had come. She felt too lonely and unhappy.

'Cheer up,' whispered Dad as the service ended. 'Everyone wants to meet us now. Don't let them see that gloomy face, will you?'

'I don't want to meet anyone,' Rosie pouted. 'There isn't anyone to be friends with.'

'Lots of people will want to be friends,' Dad promised. 'Just wait and see.'

'But there aren't any girls my age,' she hissed. 'Not one.'

'Friends can be any age,' Dad said, 'young or old. And the church is God's family, remember, and lots of

20

people will want to be friendly. Perhaps you can help someone else today who is lonely and shy.'

'I don't think so,' Rosie said.

'Jesus will help you,' Dad told her. 'Just ask him.'

Mum and Dad were talking for a very long time. Rosie smiled at everyone who came to say 'hello' to her, but inside she felt very unhappy. She wished she could go home.

While she was waiting, she noticed that a girl with long, fair hair was busy collecting up books. She was much older than Rosie, almost a grown-up, but Rosie remembered how much better she'd felt the day before when she'd helped Mum instead of doing nothing. So she began to collect the books near her and took them to the cupboard, just as the girl was doing.

'That's nice of you,' the older girl said with a shy smile. 'Your name is Rosie, isn't it? I'm Debbie Watts.'

'I'm waiting for my mum and dad,' Rosie said. 'Are you waiting for yours?'

'No,' said Debbie. 'I don't live with my mum and dad. I've just moved here too a few weeks ago and I live on my own.'

Rosie gasped again. She suddenly realized that Jesus had helped her! She was making friends with someone else who was shy and lonely. She rushed to ask Mum and Dad if Debbie could come home with them.

And she did. She stayed until Rosie went to bed and was the best friend that Rosie could possibly have dreamed of having. They went out for a walk together in the afternoon. Debbie showed her a little park where the trees and bushes reminded her of the home she had just left. To find so many flowers growing, row upon row, like a hundred beautiful gardens together, cheered her up so that she smiled and chatted gaily to Debbie all the way home.

As she went home, Debbie said, 'Thank you for a lovely day. I've enjoyed myself so much.'

'I'm glad you came,' said Mum. 'We all are, especially Rosie. Come as often as you like.'

'You were right, Dad,' said Rosie later when he kissed her goodnight. 'Friends can be any age.'

Changes

On Monday morning, Rosie and Mark started their new schools. They both felt strange at first, especially Rosie who didn't have a friend to go with.

Mark, of course, went with Sadhu and soon knew everything there was to know about the school.

And, in just a few days, Rosie too had made friends and felt quite happy at school.

In only a few weeks, both Mark and Rosie had settled down. It was just as Dad had said, they liked their new house, their new school, their new church and their new friends. Rosie even stopped noticing how ugly the streets were and how plain the houses were. Now she noticed other things like people's smiles, a pretty window box and a cat sitting on a window sill.

Then, things began to change again. They had known for a long time that, one day, they would have a new baby in the family, but it hadn't made much difference to them. It had only meant that Mum had to be more careful about what she ate and more careful about what she did. But now big changes were happening.

One day, Mark took Sadhu into Mum and Dad's bedroom to show him what was going on.

'Look,' he said, 'they've put the cot up now and got all my baby things out. Our baby's going to be born soon.'

Sadhu laughed. 'Your baby things?'

''Cos I was the last baby in this family!' Mark explained. 'So I wore them all last.'

'Oh yes,' said Sadhu, 'I forgot.' He had two little sisters and a baby brother himself, so it seemed funny to him that Mark, who was the same age, had been the last baby. He picked up a tiny yellow baby suit that was lying on the bed. 'Funny baby clothes,' he said. 'Our baby has proper clothes to wear, not like these.'

Mark glared at him. 'These *are* proper baby clothes.'

Sadhu held up the yellow suit, making a face as he looked at it. 'My mum doesn't put our baby in that sort of thing. It would look silly.'

Mark leaned forward to grab the suit, but Sadhu snatched it away. That made Mark fall. He grabbed the bed cover and landed with a bump on the floor, pulling the cover and all the piles of baby clothes, sheets, nappies and blankets on top of him. Sadhu stood staring, his brown eyes wide with horror.

Rosie heard the bump and ran in to see what had happened. She gave a gasp. 'Look what you've done!' she cried. 'Mum'll be furious with you!'

He leapt up, scattering things left and right. 'It wasn't my fault!' he yelled. 'It was Sadhu.'

'Sadhu's not doing anything,' Rosie said. 'It's you who's messing up everything. Sadhu's just standing there.'

Mark's face was hot and red. 'He started it!' he screamed.

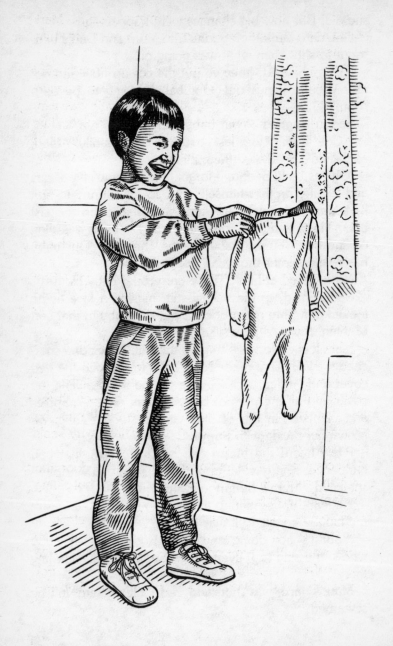

Just then, they heard Mum coming upstairs. Mark pulled a face and pushed out his lips in a pout. He knew he was going to be in trouble.

'What's all the noise?' Mum demanded. 'You knew I was trying to have a rest. Why can't you play quietly?' And then she saw what had happened. She was very cross. 'What have you been doing?' she shouted. 'I've been working very hard to get all those things washed and ironed and ready to go away in the drawers. Now I'm going to have to start all over again. What were you all doing in here, anyway? You've got your own bedrooms to play in, haven't you?'

She picked up the whole bed cover and took all the clothes downstairs in it. Mark felt horrible. He stuck out his tongue at Rosie.

'I didn't do anything!' said Rosie. 'It was you.' She flounced out, leaving Mark with Sadhu. Mark was afraid that Sadhu would laugh or tease him, so he glared at his friend, but Sadhu felt embarrassed.

'I think my mum will want me now,' said Sadhu. 'I'd better go home.' And away he went, padding quickly and quietly down the stairs. The front door banged.

Mark sat on the floor. Why is Mum so cross all the time? he wondered. She never used to be. It must be the baby that makes her so grumpy. That's why she's changed.

He crept downstairs and peeped around the door into the living room. Mum was there, not ironing, but sitting still, looking tired.

'Mum,' he began in a little voice, just a bit afraid in case she was still cross. 'I'm sorry.'

She opened her arms so that he could tuck in beside her on the chair. He began to feel much better. For a little while, he stayed there, happy to be quiet and comfortable.

Then he said, 'Mum, when the baby's born, do you think we'd better give it away?'

'Why ever should we want to do that?' she asked. 'That's a silly thing to say.'

'Well,' he explained, 'if the baby makes you change and be cross all the time with me and Rosie, then we're going to be sad all the time.'

For a while, Mark thought Mum hadn't heard. He was just going to say it all again, when she gave him a little squeeze. 'Oh Mark, I'm sorry, too, if I've been cross all the time. But I'm not cross because I'm having a baby. I'm just tired, that's all. There's been so much work to do lately and carrying the baby with me all the time is hard work too.'

'Will it be all right again when the baby's born, then?' he asked. 'You won't be cross all the time for ever?'

Mum laughed. 'Of course not, love. Once the baby's here and settled into the family, things will get better again. And I don't have to be cross when I'm tired. I think I'd better ask God to help me, don't you?'

Mark was quiet again for a few minutes. He was enjoying the sleepy cuddle with Mum, but a thought in his mind wouldn't let him alone.

'I think,' he said at last, 'I'd better ask God to help me be good. Then you won't have to get cross so much.'

'Good idea,' said Mum. 'Let's both have a talk to him.'

The family service

'We can't go to church today!' cried Mark suddenly.

'Don't be silly, Mark,' said Dad impatiently. 'Of course we can!'

'No, but it's a family service,' Mark said, 'like the first time we went when we'd just moved here. So, this time, we can't go, can we?'

'Eat your breakfast up,' snapped Dad, 'and stop talking nonsense. We'll be late if you don't hurry up.'

Mark stared at his plate. Rosie had burnt the toast. Dad had let the baked beans go hard and dry in the saucepan. 'I'm not hungry,' he grumbled.

'Go and brush your hair, then,' said Dad. 'We'd better get ready.'

Mark climbed the stairs. It's not fair, he thought. I wish Mum was here instead of being in hospital. Then we'd be a proper family again. We can't go to a family service without Mum.

Rosie and Mark's mum had had to go to hospital the day before. It was nearly time for the baby to be born and Mum had been getting very tired. The doctor had sent her to hospital for a rest. Mark missed her very much.

He brushed his curly hair, looking into his mirror. What a gloomy face he had! It wasn't surprising. Breakfast had been horrible. And now they were going to look silly at the family service!

The church building was full of people. Sunshine was making the coloured glass shine brightly in the windows.

'All things bright and beautiful, all creatures great and small,' they sang.

Rosie and Dad joined in, but Mark didn't, although it was one of his favourite songs. He kept thinking, 'Everyone must be laughing at us.'

During the prayers, when he thought no one might be looking at him, he turned around to look behind him.

Sadhu's got his mum and his dad here, he thought. He's got his aunt and uncle too and his sisters and baby brother. I bet he's laughing at us.

He turned further round. Joe Andrews and his mum are here – but he hasn't got a dad. That's funny!

He twisted round to face another way. Old Miss Richardson isn't married, but she's come. Debbie Watts is here on her own, too!

He wriggled round and faced the front again. He began to wonder whether Mr Taplow, the pastor, knew that half the people in the family service weren't families at all. Then he thought, even Mr and Mrs Taplow shouldn't be here! They haven't got any children!

He nudged Dad and whispered, 'This is all wrong, Dad.'

'Shh!' hissed Dad.

'I want to tell you something!' he insisted.

'Later,' whispered Dad.

'I want to tell you now,' he said. He spoke very loudly,

much louder than he'd meant to. Suddenly, everyone was looking at Mark, smiling. Mark went red and very quiet.

'Everyone laughed at me,' he grumbled afterwards, as they walked home together.

Rosie giggled. 'You were funny, though, Mark, shouting out like that in the middle of the prayers!'

'Nobody meant to be unkind,' comforted Dad, patting Mark's shoulder. 'People understand how hard it is to keep quiet for long at your age.'

'We should never have gone in the first place,' said Mark to himself.

Breakfast had been horrible, but their dinner was wonderful! Mrs Ram came round with a pot full of curry and some fried rice.

'I would have invited you to our home, but with my sister and her family here it would be so crowded. But I've made you a special mild curry so you won't burn your mouths. I hope you like it.'

And they did!

Mrs Taplow had baked them a huge cherry pie which they ate afterwards. Mark had three slices and began to feel much better than he had all morning.

'People are so kind,' said Dad as he pushed back his chair. 'It's great belonging to God's family.'

Mark stared at him. 'God's family?' he asked. 'What's that?'

'Why, we are!' cried Dad. 'You, me, Rosie and Mum are part of God's family and so are all the other people all over the world who love God and follow Jesus.'

Mark jumped up. 'Oh, I see! That's why we had a family service, is it?'

'Yes,' laughed Dad. 'Didn't you know?'

'I thought it was just for mums and dads and children,'

he said. 'But really it's for everyone in God's family, isn't it?'

'Yes,' said Dad. 'And anyone can belong to God's family if they want to – anyone at all.'

Mark thought about it. Debbie and Miss Richardson, Mr and Mrs Taplow, Joe Andrews and his mum, the Rams and their relatives. They'd only known them all a few weeks, but all the time they had been in the same family as him and he hadn't even known it!'

'Does Mum know about God's family?' he asked.

'Yes,' Dad told him. 'That's why she was happy to move here. She knew we'd find some of our family here. Not Gran or your aunts and uncles, but people in God's family who love God just like we do.'

'Shall we go and see her now?' asked Rosie. 'We can tell her what a good family we've got and how they're looking after us while she's away.'

'Right,' said Dad. 'We'll clear up when we get back.'

'I can't wait to see her,' said Mark.

Proper family

'The trouble is,' thought Rosie, 'that I want Mum. I don't really want anyone else looking after us.'

'Hurry!' called Dad. 'Breakfast's ready!'

Rosie tried to hurry, but she couldn't tie her plaits. Every time she had them almost tied in the ribbons, one would come apart again. I wish Mum was here, she thought. She does this so quickly.

Dad was ready to go to work when she got downstairs. 'Now remember,' he told the children, 'Mrs Andrews will be here soon to get you off to school. Mark, you go home with Sadhu after school and Rosie, you go along to Miss Richardson's.'

'Do I have to?' asked Rosie.

'Yes, she's expecting you,' said Dad. 'But Debbie will be here this evening. She'll put you to bed while I go and see Mum. You like Debbie, don't you?'

Rosie wanted to cry. She liked Debbie, but it wasn't the same as having Mum.

'Cheer up,' said Dad. 'It's only for today. Gran is

coming tomorrow.'

'At least Gran's my proper family,' said Rosie, but Dad didn't hear. He had to hurry off to work, leaving Mark and Rosie alone. They felt very strange.

In a few minutes, just as they were finishing their breakfast, Mrs Andrews came in with Joe, who was two years younger than Mark. The two boys ran upstairs to play. Rosie was left with Mrs Andrews. She began to feel very shy. She didn't know Mrs Andrews very well and wasn't sure what to say to her.

'Let's clear the table,' suggested Mrs Andrews.

'Dad said he'd do it later,' Rosie told her, not looking up.

'We'll give him a nice surprise, then, shall we?' asked Mrs Andrews. 'Are you going to give me a hand?'

Rosie looked up and noticed how kind her smile was, so she nodded and they began to work. In a while, the table was empty and the kitchen spotlessly clean.

'Now,' said Mrs Andrews, 'is there anything else I can help with before you go to school?'

'Well, my plaits won't tie up,' Rosie said, holding up her messy brown hair to show her.

Mrs Andrews laughed. 'No trouble,' she said. 'I used to have plaits too when I was your age, so I know how hard it can be to tie them up yourself. You just run and get your brush and we'll fix them up in no time.'

As Mrs Andrews deftly plaited her hair, Rosie thought what a nice person Joe's mum was.

There was still something for Rosie to worry about, though. After school, she had to go to Miss Richardson's house. It was only a few streets away from home, but Rosie had been there only once before. Dad had taken her the day before but Rosie kept worrying that she would forget the way. And, of course, she was worrying about Miss Richardson too. She seemed very old, even

older than Gran. Gran's hair was going grey, but Miss Richardson's was snowy white and pinned up in the old-fashioned way which made her seem very old indeed. What would they say to each other until Dad came to collect her?

It was easy to find the right house. That was one worry over, but as Miss Richardson led her along the hallway to her back room, Rosie wished that she could have gone to tea with one of her friends instead. But Dad had said that he hadn't had time to make any other arrangements.

'Come in, Rosie,' said Miss Richardson. She was tall and straight for an old person, but walking to the door and back seemed to have made her tired. She sat down by the fireplace with a sigh. 'Tea's all ready,' she told her with a smile.

Miss Richardson's room was full of wonders. Rosie's eyes wandered around the room as she munched at the delicious chocolate cake that Miss Richardson had made.

'I'll show you some of my treasures after tea,' the old lady promised. 'I was born in China, you know, and some of the things were my parents'. That makes them pretty old, doesn't it?'

'Are you Chinese, then?' asked Rosie.

Miss Richardson laughed. 'No, I'm not, Rosie, but my parents were missionaries out there when I was born.'

'Missionaries?' asked Rosie.

'Telling people about Jesus,' explained Miss Richardson. 'And they were running a little medical clinic to help people who were ill.'

'Can you remember it?' asked Rosie.

And Miss Richardson began to tell Rosie all about the long ago days when she was a child in a huge country where so many people live that it seemed you were never on your own.

It wasn't until they heard a knock on the door that Rosie realized how long she had been there. And she had been worried about what she and Miss Richardson would talk about!

She put down the ivory chopsticks that Miss Richardson had been showing her and glanced at the clock.

'I expect that's your father,' Miss Richardson said as she struggled out of her chair. 'And we've hardly begun to look at all my treasures. You'll have to come again, Rosie. I've enjoyed myself so much.'

'Can I go and see Miss Richardson again soon?' asked Rosie as she walked home with Dad.

'Of course,' he said. 'Did you have a good time?'

'Yes!' she cried. 'She was really kind, Dad, and so was Joe's mum this morning. I thought I'd hate being with people who weren't my proper family, but I didn't!'

'Well,' said Dad, 'it's hard to understand, but they *are* our family. We're all part of God's family.'

'We still have to get to know them first, though, don't we?' said Rosie. 'But once you do, it does feel like family, but I'll still be glad when Gran comes tomorrow.'

'Of course,' said Dad. 'You know her better. It's nice to have an extra family, though, isn't it?'

As Rosie untied her plaits that evening, she smiled. How miserable she'd been that morning when she'd tried to tie them up. She was much happier now! Of course, she still wished Mum was at home, but she'd found that she could enjoy being with other people too. They were her proper family – and she had started to love them. They had helped her and she began to wish that she could help them.

There was busy Mrs Andrews. Perhaps I could do some shopping for her sometimes, she thought.

What about Miss Richardson? I bet she gets lonely,

she thought. I'll ask Mum and Dad to let me go and see her sometimes.

And Debbie Watts was waiting downstairs to read her and Mark a story before bedtime. What could I do for her? she wondered. I think she just likes being friends!

Then she brushed her hair, pushed her feet into her old, comfortable slippers and ran down to enjoy being with Mark and Debbie.

The bike

'Mark, it's mine!' shouted Rosie, pulling her bicycle away from her brother.

Mark held on. 'It's not fair!' he yelled back. 'I haven't got a bike.'

'You have,' said Rosie.

'I haven't.'

'Yes, you have,' she repeated, tugging at the handle-bars. 'Give mine back. I want to ride it now.'

Mark pulled so hard that they toppled over with the bike between them.

'It's your fault,' Mark cried. 'You won't share. You know my bike is too small for me.'

Rosie was nursing a scraped knee. 'Leave my bike alone!' she shouted. 'There's nothing wrong with your bike.'

'Except it's too small and too old,' he muttered as he crawled out from under the wheels.

Just then, Gran trudged out from the house. She'd only arrived the day before. She looked cross, with a

frown on her small round face that drew her eyebrows down over her twinkly eyes, and made her look just like Dad when he was annoyed. The children had forgotten that she liked a sit-down in the afternoon.

'You're making far too much noise,' she told them, helping Rosie to pick up the bike. 'You'll disturb all the neighbours.'

'It's her fault!' began Mark.

'He took my bike without asking!' Rosie said at the same time.

Gran shook her head. 'Come in, both of you,' she said. She sounded stern, but she stopped to wave cheerfully at little Joe Andrews. He had been watching Rosie and Mark from the other side of the street. Gran led them inside. Mark pulled a rude face at Rosie as they followed. Rosie pulled a rude face back.

'Well,' said Gran, sitting at the kitchen table, 'this reminds me of something. Sit down, stop making faces and I'll tell you.'

They sat down. Gran handed round some biscuits. She washed Rosie's scraped knee and then she began her story.

'When I was a girl, my sisters and I were always fighting just like you do. And one of the things we fought over was my doll. We didn't have many toys, you see, but I had a beautiful doll that my godmother had given me. She had a wax face and a soft yellow dress, I remember. I wouldn't share her with anyone. I was afraid, you see, that my sisters would spoil her. They thought I was very mean.

'Then, one Sunday in church, we heard about some children who would have no Christmas presents that year. They were living in a children's home – what we used to call an orphanage – and had no families of their own to buy presents for them. We were told to bring toys to church next Sunday if we wanted to give one of those children a present.

'Of course, we all wanted to, but what could we give? We were quite poor ourselves. So I asked Mother and guess what she said? "Ask God to give you an idea!" So, when I said my prayers that night I asked God what I could give. Before long, I thought of something.'

'Oh, Gran,' said Rosie, 'not your beautiful doll?'

'Yes,' she said. 'I kept thinking of it. I loved that doll so much, but I knew I was much luckier than those children who had no families. So, next Sunday, I took my doll to church and put her under the Christmas tree.'

'Did you cry?' asked Rosie.

'A little bit, but I was very happy too. I was glad I'd done it.'

'What happened?' asked Mark.

Gran smiled. 'Well, I stopped arguing with my sisters over the doll. Wasn't that a good thing?'

'Is that why you told us the story?' asked Rosie.

Gran nodded. 'Well, it seems a shame. You've got so many toys – and you spend all your time fighting over them. Couldn't you think of something better?'

'Like what?' they asked.

Gran smiled. 'Ask God to give you an idea,' she said. 'Now, go and play. I'd better get some supper. Your dad will be home soon.'

'I don't think Joe Andrews has got a bike at all,' said Mark a little later as they played in the back garden.

'His mum can't afford one, I expect,' said Rosie.

'We've got two,' Mark said, 'only mine is a bit too small.'

'If we shared mine,' Rosie suggested, 'we wouldn't need your old one.'

Mark kicked his ball against the fence and watched it fall into the long grass under the trees. 'Joe could have my bike,' he said. 'Do you think that's a good idea, Rosie?'

She nodded. 'We'll have to ask Mum and Dad if it's all right. I'm sure they'll let us, though.'

On Sunday, after church service, Joe's mum said to Rosie and Mark, 'Joe's so pleased with that bike you gave him. He's riding it the whole time, now. Thank you for giving it to him. It was really nice of you.'

'It was Mark's idea, really,' Rosie said.

'But I liked giving it to Joe,' he said. 'It made me happy!'

And it was true!

The obstacle course

Dad was tired. 'Will you be quiet?' he yelled. 'We're trying to watch the news!'

Gran was tired too. 'Go and play somewhere else, Mark. You've been under my feet all day.'

Mark pushed out a sulky lip. 'It's not fair,' he said.

'There's lots of room to play upstairs,' Dad told him. 'I want a bit of peace and quiet before we go out and see Mum.'

Mark looked sadly at his game. He had just got it all set up. His plastic astronauts were about to explore a new planet – his football, really. They had only just landed and now Dad and Gran wanted him to stop the game. He knew that the commands he'd been shouting from Earth control centre had been a bit loud, but it didn't seem fair.

He thought, Dad and Gran are horrible. Mean and horrible. He frowned and went outside. It was raining a little. There was no one else in the street.

He called into the house, 'Can I go and play with

Sadhu?'

Dad said he could. So Mark crossed the street and knocked at the Rams' house.

Sadhu was pleased to see him. 'Come and see what I've made in our bedroom,' he told his friend. 'It's an obstacle course,' he explained as they went in.

There were chairs to climb over and under, plastic bottles to weave in and out of, pillows to leap across, a blanket to wriggle under.

'You end up,' explained Sadhu, 'by climbing up the ladder to the top bunk and jumping across to my bed. See?'

Mark nodded. It looked fun.

'Give me your watch and I'll time you,' said Sadhu. 'Then you can time me.'

'I bet I'll be faster than you,' boasted Mark.

But it was harder than he'd thought. He got stuck going under a chair and had to start again when he knocked over some bottles.

'Two minutes, twenty-eight seconds,' called Sadhu as Mark hit the bed with a bump. 'That's really slow. Now watch me go!'

Mark took his watch back angrily. Sadhu went very fast. He'd been practising and didn't get stuck anywhere. He wriggled under the chairs at top speed. But, as he landed on the bed, Mark said, 'Two minutes, forty seconds.'

'It was not!' shouted Sadhu.

'It was!' insisted Mark, who didn't want to lose.

'It must have been one minute, forty seconds,' Sadhu said. 'I didn't have to start again.'

'I just did everything faster than you,' lied Mark.

They glared at each other. Sadhu yelled, 'You cheat!'

'I am not!' replied Mark, going red. He stomped out of the room and went downstairs and out into the rain.

He was crossing the road, when he remembered he'd forgotten his jumper.

He stood in the street, wondering what to do next. 'They don't want me at home,' he thought, 'and I can't go back to Sadhu's.'

Then he realized how stupid he'd been.

I should have let him win, he told himself. He *was* faster than me.

A shout made him turn.

'You forgot something!' The Rams' door slammed and Sadhu came running out with Mark's red jumper.

Mark took it. 'You did win, really,' he said.

'I know,' said Sadhu, 'but I'd been practising and the chair was too small for you to get through. It's not your fault I'm so thin, is it?'

It was good to be friends again. They smiled.

'Come and try the obstacle course again?' suggested Sadhu.

Mark shook his head. 'Better not. It hurt when I landed on your bed, but you can come and play my game, if you like.'

The news on television was over. Dad and Gran were in the kitchen.

'Sorry for spoiling your game,' said Dad as they came in. 'We didn't mean to upset you.'

Mark knew just how to make things better quickly. Sadhu had shown him how to do it.

'I was being noisy,' he admitted. 'Sorry. Is it all right if we play the game now?'

'Of course,' said Dad with a smile. 'It must be a long way from Earth to that new planet they've discovered. You would have to shout commands, I suppose, but don't make it too loud, will you?'

Baby Alice

One day, not long after, Rosie was telling her new friends at school, 'I've got a baby sister. She's called Alice. We're going to see her straight after school.'

The next day, she told them, 'Alice is really tiny. Mum let me stroke her cheeks and hold her hand.'

The following day, she was even more excited. 'Mum's bringing Alice home today. I'm going to hold her all by myself and give her a cuddle.'

What a long day it seemed to Rosie. It was hard to get her work done, but at last school was over. Rosie ran home as fast as she could.

'Where's Alice?' she asked Gran as soon as she opened the door.

'In the garden, having a sleep,' she said. 'Your mum's there, too, with Mark. Go and see them.'

Rosie ran out to hug Mum. It was lovely to have her home again. 'Can I cuddle Alice now?' she asked.

'Not yet, Rosie,' said Mum. 'She's rather unsettled. I've only just got her off to sleep. I don't want to risk waking her now.'

Rosie was disappointed. 'Oh, please,' she begged.

'No,' said Mum. 'Just be patient. Wait until she wakes up next.'

It was hard to be patient. Rosie had already waited all day to hold Alice, but at least she could look at the baby as much as she liked. She carefully stroked Alice's silky hair with one finger, standing guard over the pram so that Mark wouldn't get to the baby first when she woke up.

'I hope she wakes up soon,' she thought as she looked at her new sister.

Mum thought differently. She was glad that Alice was having a long sleep. 'It's hard work having a tiny baby,' she told the children. 'I'm glad to have a rest – and some time with you two. I've missed you, you know, while I've been in hospital.'

It was nearly Rosie's bedtime when Alice began to cry.

'She's very hungry,' Mum said. 'Just hold her for a moment, Rosie.'

But Alice wriggled and kicked so hard that Mum was afraid that Rosie would drop her. 'I'd better feed her at once,' she said. 'I'm sorry, Rosie. You'll get a chance to cuddle her tomorrow.'

Rosie tried hard to hide how upset she was. After all, she realized that Alice was very hungry. Now she would have to be patient even longer!

In the morning, everything was running late.

'Alice was awake half the night,' Gran told the children. 'Your dad's had to go to work without any breakfast and Mum is still asleep. Don't disturb her, will you?'

Alice was asleep too. How disappointing! Rosie had to wait again. The school day seemed longer than ever.

When she got home, Mark was in a mood, Alice was

crying and Mum was looking tired.

'Just wait until Gran gets back from the shops,' Mum was saying to Mark. 'I've got my hands full looking after Alice.'

'I told Sadhu I'd get my football at once,' Mark shouted. 'I can't find it and he's waiting!'

'He can wait a few minutes, surely,' snapped Mum.

Rosie put down her school bag. 'I'll help you, Mark,' she said. Together they searched the dark cupboard under the stairs.

'It's not fair,' said Mark. 'Mum doesn't care about us. All she cares about is that baby.'

'Don't be silly,' replied Rosie. 'Of course she cares about us. But we can do things for ourselves and Alice can't. And we can be patient and Alice can't yet.'

'I can't either!' said Mark angrily. 'I want Mum to help me look for my football.'

'But Mum's busy and tired,' pleaded Rosie. 'Look, here's your football. You can't have looked very hard.'

Mark grabbed the ball, pouted and went outside. Rosie went to sit beside Mum, watching her feed Alice.

'When can I hold her, Mum?' asked Rosie.

'Very soon, now,' promised Mum. 'Thank you for being so patient.'

'It's not very easy,' she said.

'I know,' replied Mum. 'Patience doesn't come easily. It's something we have to learn. And we are all going to have to ask God to help us to be extra patient with each other for a while until Alice settles in.'

'Especially Mark,' Rosie said. 'He's horrible!'

'Yes,' laughed Mum, 'and we'll have to be patient with him, too. Baby Alice has changed everything and Mark will find it hard to get used to all the changes.'

Now, at last, Alice was ready. Mum put her into her sister's lap. Rosie held her gently. 'This is what I wanted

all along,' she said happily.

It took a while to get used to the proper way to hold Alice because her neck seemed so floppy and Rosie felt stiff and awkward. But that didn't last long. Then she found how to hold her firmly but carefully and have one hand free to stroke her sister's downy head.

'She hasn't got much hair,' Rosie said.

'It'll grow soon,' Mum told her. 'I know she looks a bit funny at the moment, though.'

Rosie looked down proudly at Alice. 'I don't think she looks funny at all,' she said. 'I think she's the most beautiful baby in the world and I love her.'

It's not fair

It didn't seem fair to Mark. Before Alice was born, he had been the youngest. If the family had had to wait for anyone, it had been him. For instance, if he had been slow tying up his shoelaces, then the whole family would have to wait before they could go out together. And if it had taken him a long time to get ready for school, then someone would usually help him, just to hurry him up.

Suddenly, things like that didn't happen any more. If anyone needed waiting for, it was Alice.

'Oh, we can't go out yet,' Mum would say. 'Alice hasn't had her feed. Go and play for a while, Mark. I'll let you know when we're going.'

And, when he was getting ready for school, nobody would notice that he couldn't find his spelling book or whether he'd remembered to collect his lunch from the kitchen. Mum was too busy with Alice. He had to think of everything himself.

Sometimes, of course, Alice was asleep in her pram, but then Mum had so many things to do, like tidying the house, washing up, ironing and cooking. She didn't seem to have time to help him look for the game he wanted from the back of his toy cupboard or the book he'd been reading the night before.

It just wasn't fair! But whenever Alice cried, Mum would go and see what she wanted. And whenever a visitor came, it was to see Alice and they hardly noticed him at all.

'What a happy boy you must be,' they might say to him as they passed him.

But Mark didn't feel very happy. He liked Alice, but he did feel cross with her sometimes.

Until Gran had gone home, it hadn't been too bad. Gran had done most of the work around the house. But now that Mum was doing it herself, there didn't seem much time for anything else, except Alice. Mark tried not to be grumpy, but it was difficult.

Then, one Saturday, Dad said, 'There's a work party at church today. Would you like to come?'

Mark liked all sorts of parties, but he'd never heard of a work party, so he just frowned.

'It's just a few of us helping to get the church clean and tidy,' Dad explained. 'I'm going to help for a few hours and I thought you'd like to come.'

Mark wasn't sure. He didn't think he'd like doing lots of work, but he did like going out with Dad, so he nodded.

He was glad that Rosie was staying at home with Mum and Alice. It was nice to go somewhere by himself with Dad.

At first, he just watched while Dad and some other people tidied up the garden in front of the church building.

Then he began to get bored and went indoors. He found Mr Taplow in the big hall where the youth club met on Friday nights. He was looking in a huge cupboard, shaking his head.

'What's all that stuff?' asked Mark, seeing what was in the cupboard. He'd never seen such a muddle in all his life!

'It's the youth club cupboard,' said Mr Taplow. 'I've been meaning to turn it out for a very long time. None of the young people has come to help this morning, so I suppose I'd better begin on my own.'

'I could help,' said Mark eagerly.

It was wonderful fun! There were all kinds of interesting things in that cupboard – badminton rackets, compasses, cricket bats, ropes and pulleys, a folding stretcher and even a crash helmet. Mark tried the helmet on. It was so heavy he thought his head was going to fall off!

'Well, I think some of this could be thrown away,' said Mr Taplow. 'I'll go and find some rubbish bags, Mark, and you can start putting this pile of things back neatly into the cupboard.'

When Mr Taplow got back with some black plastic sacks, Mark had nearly finished. The cupboard was so tidy that you could easily find anything you wanted.

'Well done, Mark,' said Mr Taplow. 'I can see you're a good worker. Your mum and dad must be proud of you.'

Mark was pleased that Mr Taplow thought so, but he felt ashamed all the same. He knew that he wasn't a good worker at home. In fact, he knew that he was lazy. He didn't do any work at all if he thought someone else would do it for him.

He was very quiet as he walked home with Dad later.

'Has all that work made you so tired?' asked Dad. 'You haven't said a word.'

'No, I'm not tired,' said Mark, 'just thinking.'

'OK,' said Dad, 'but you can tell me about it if you

like.'

'No,' Mark replied. 'It's not a telling thing. It's a doing thing. Something I'm going to do.'

And Mark began to do all sorts of things. He tidied his own bedroom and made it as tidy as the youth club cupboard, so that you could find anything you wanted. Then he wasn't so slow getting ready for school because he knew where his shoes were and where his spelling book was.

And he didn't need Mum to help him so much because he began to do things for himself. It made him feel much better. He didn't mind Alice needing Mum so much. He knew that he was bigger and cleverer than she was.

But when he did need Mum or Dad to help with things he really couldn't do himself, they would always be there.

And, when people said to him, 'What a happy boy you must be now that you have a little baby sister,' he began to think that it wasn't so bad, after all.

A party for Alice

'We're going to have a party!' sang Rosie.
'We're going to have an enormous tea!
We're going to have a party,
All for me!'
'All for Alice,' Mark corrected.
'I know,' said Rosie, 'but that doesn't go into the tune so well.'

Baby Alice was growing up fast. She was still only a few weeks old, but she could smile – and she didn't cry as much. When Rosie or Mark talked to her, she made funny sounds, trying to talk back.

It was Sunday. There was going to be a special service at church for Alice. Afterwards, lots of friends were coming home for tea.

The house was already full of busy people. Miss Richardson, who had arrived wearing a new red hat and coat, was putting cakes and sandwiches on to plates. Debbie, her long fair hair tied back in a big white bow, was setting out cups and saucers. Mrs Ram, wearing a special sari, was arranging vases of flowers from her garden.

Meanwhile Dad, looking extra smart in his best suit, was tidying the house. Mum had a new dress upstairs, but wasn't going to put it on until she had finished feeding Alice. Mark and Rosie, taking great care not to spill anything on the matching green jumpers that Gran had knitted for them, were busy carrying plates and knives, bowls and plates from the kitchen to the tables which had been set up in the front room.

'We're going to have a party!' sang Rosie – and Mark joined in too. 'We're going to have a party – all for me!'

'Did you have a party for me,' asked Mark, 'when I was a baby, I mean?'

'Yes,' said Mum, 'but not such a big one. We didn't know so many people then. This party is to say thank-you to all the people who have helped us since we came to live here.'

When it was nearly time to go to church, people began to leave. Mum took off Alice's stripey blue stretch suit and put her in a pretty white dress. Mark and Rosie stood and watched.

'I can't wait for the party!' Mark said, glancing at the table. 'Just look at all those cakes Miss Richardson made!'

'Greedy boy!' teased Dad. He perched on the arm of Mum's chair. 'You know, the party will be fun, but the time at church is more important. It will be a chance to say a special thank-you to God for giving us Alice. And we – Mum and I, and the rest of our church family – are going to make promises.'

'Promise what?' asked Rosie, stroking Alice's soft hair.

'We're going to promise to help Alice to learn about God and to get to know him for herself.'

Mark laughed. 'That's silly, though. She doesn't even know what we're talking about yet.'

'She will one day,' Mum said. 'But we can help her learn about God before then, you know.'

'How?' asked the children.

'By being patient and kind and loving,' Mum explained. 'When she sees us trying to be like Jesus, she'll begin to understand something about what God is like. And she'll see us praying and find out how important God is to us.'

'That's how you two began to learn about God,' Dad reminded them.

The party was going well. Even Mark had eaten enough cakes and he sat down to wait for Sadhu who was having a look at Alice.

'Are you enjoying yourself?' asked Miss Richardson, who was sitting next to Mark.

He nodded. 'I liked the bit in the service when we all promised to help Alice learn about God, but the food was my real favourite.'

'I thought so,' said Miss Richardson.

'You know,' Mark said, 'me and Rosie are going to teach Alice about God too. We're going to help her understand about how good and patient and kind he is. Dad said so.'

Miss Richardson smiled. 'Good,' she said, 'but, Mark, don't forget to go on learning yourself, will you? I've been a Christian a long time and I'm still learning, you know.'

Mark stared. 'You must know nearly everything, though,' he said.

She laughed, softly, shaking her head. 'Oh, I'm not so very old, Mark,' she said.

'I didn't really mean that,' said Mark blushing.

'No, I know,' said Miss Richardson and Mark knew that she wasn't upset or cross. 'You know,' she went on seriously, 'God's so great and so wonderful, Mark, there's always something new to find out. Even if I was two hundred years old, I'd still be finding out new things about him.'

Mark's eyes grew big. He was wondering how old Miss Richardson could possibly be, though he knew it wasn't polite to ask. Could she be one hundred years old?

'And, you know,' Miss Richardson went on, 'we can all learn from each other in God's family. The young ones teach the old ones, too!'

'Really?' said Mark in great surprise. 'Give you lessons, you mean?'

'No,' she laughed. 'Just by the things you do and the things you say. By the way you trust God so simply without asking lots of silly grown-up questions.'

What a very surprising person Miss Richardson was! Mark hadn't really talked to her before, but he was beginning to like her very much.

'Wow!' he cried, 'I never knew I was that important!'

'Everyone is,' she replied. 'Look around at all the lovely people here – all your friends – Joe and his mum, Sadhu and his family, young Debbie and kind Mr and Mrs Taplow, your family, even little baby Alice and all the others – they're all important. God loves every single one. That's the most important thing that could ever happen to anyone. It makes us all special, doesn't it?'

'Yes,' said Mark happily. 'It does.'